ROBOT
GIRL

Malorie
BLACKMAN

With illustrations by Matthew Griffin

www.malorieblackman.co.uk

To Neil and Lizzy
With love
As always

First published in 2015 in Great Britain by
Barrington Stoke Ltd
18 Walker Street, Edinburgh, EH3 7LP

www.barringtonstoke.co.uk

This story was first published in a different form in
Sensational Cyber Stories (Transworld, 1997)

Text © 1997 Oneta Malorie Blackman
Illustrations © 2015 Matthew Griffin

A CIP catalogue record for this book is available
from the British Library upon request

ISBN: 978-1-78112-459-8

Printed in China by Leo

CONTENTS

CHAPTER 1
DATA

"Come on, Mum, you must know."

Mum groaned. "Claire, how many more times must I tell you?" she said. "I don't know what your dad is working on. You know he doesn't like to show us a project until it's finished and he's happy with it. It has to be perfect before he'll let anyone else in the lab."

"But what d'you think it might be?" I asked. "I mean, why did he need all that data about me? Like how long my fingers are and how far I can see and how tall I am and all that?

And why did he scan my mind for my brain patterns? What's that got to do with ...?"

"Claire, read my lips – I don't know." Mum raised a hand to swot away a fly that was buzzing around her. She made contact and it fell dead at her feet.

I decided not to push my luck. It was clear that Mum was getting more than a little annoyed. She almost had sparks flying out of her eyes.

"Look, Claire," Mum said, "your dad said he'd show us his project later today and he will. Until then you'll just have to wait." She seemed a bit calmer now. She picked up the fly and dropped it into the bin by her chair.

I stood up.

"Where are you going?" Mum asked.

"To do my homework."

"To do your homework or to play on the net?" Mum asked.

"I don't play on the net," I told her. "I work, I study, I gather data, I support my learning ..."

"But most of the time you play!" Mum said with a laugh.

I had to laugh too – because it was true!

"Well, I'm not going to play now," I said. "I'm going to talk to my pen pal."

"You've found one at last, have you?" Mum asked.

"Mum, where've you been?" I said. "I've had a pen pal for three weeks now. Her name is Maisie. And we've got so many things in common. It's amazing."

"What about all the other people who messaged you?" Mum asked.

"It's all right," I said. "I told them that I've found a pen pal and I only want one for the time being."

"I hope you were polite," Mum said.

"Always!" I said. "You know me!"

CHAPTER 2
STUCK-UP

I tried to ignore Mum's snort of laughter behind me as I ran up to my room.

I couldn't wait to talk to Maisie again. To tell the truth, I don't have many friends.

Most of the kids in my class think I'm a bit stuck-up. They think I fancy myself. I don't. I promise I don't. I'm just a bit shy. And sometimes that makes me appear rude. But everyone has heard of my dad. He's famous. And so they think that I think I'm too good for them. That couldn't be further from the truth, but no one in my class has spent enough time with me to find out.

I mean, I'm proud of my dad, of course I am. It's just that he cares more about his work than he does about Mum and me. Mum says that's normal and I'll understand when I grow up. Somehow I don't think so.

Dad's away in his lab as often as he can manage it. I've lost count of the times I've heard Mum and Dad discuss it. They're so polite. I wish they'd have a shouting, screaming argument. At least that would be more real. But they say shouting and screaming and nonsense like that is for children, not adults. And then they say, "You'll understand when you grow up."

To be honest, I'm not sure I want to.

I needed to talk to someone about it all.

I needed to talk to Maisie.

CHAPTER 3
SISTER

To: Maisie@maisiemail.private.uk
From: Claire@clairemail.private.uk

Hi Maisie

How are you?

Dad still hasn't told us what he's working
on. The minute I know, I'll message you!
Dad always swears Mum and me to secrecy,
but you're almost like my sister, so I can
tell you. I know you won't tell anyone else.
Dad's company are so excited about this new
project – at least that's what Dad says. I'm

not surprised you've heard of my dad. He's a technology genius – at least, that's what they call him on the news.

Dad says this thing he's working on will make the kit we use now seem like "stone age tools" – his words, not mine.

I hope your dad spends more time with you than mine does with me.

Get texting. I'm waiting.

Your friend
Claire

And then the message was gone. I hoped Maisie would be online so that I'd get a message straight back. I was in luck. I didn't have long to wait.

To: Claire@clairemail.private.uk
From: Maisie@maisiemail.private.uk

Hi Claire

It's great to hear from you again. I'm glad you said what you did. To tell the truth, I think of you as a sister too.

You talk about your father as if you don't like him very much, but I envy you. I'd love a family, a real family, any kind of family. That's why it's wonderful that you want us to be as close as sisters.

I live in one room that I'm meant to call home, but it isn't – not a proper home. My father looks after me but he doesn't care about me – not about who I am inside. He just looks after me because he hopes that some day I'll make him rich. I've heard him talking to his friends about me. They all talk in front of me as if I'm deaf. I bet your father isn't like that. Write soon.

Love
Maisie

I frowned at the screen as I read Maisie's message again. I was just about to reply when Mum called me from the kitchen.

"Claire, your dad just called," she yelled. "He's at the lab and he wants us to come over as soon as we can. He's ready to show us his project."

I ran out of my bedroom. Maisie was forgotten.

"You mean we're going to see at last what he's been doing for the past year?" I said. I couldn't believe my ears. And it was odd, but even though I resented all the time Dad had spent away from us while he worked on his new project, I still couldn't wait to see it.

Mum clapped her hands. "Get your things," she said. "And remember to look impressed."

CHAPTER 4
PROJECT

"May I present AI-E, the future of technology," Dad announced. "Come on out, AI-E!"

The thing walked into the room and stood next to Dad.

"Well? What do you think?" Dad asked, with an eager grin.

I stared at Dad's latest project and felt horror bloom inside me. I couldn't help it. It was horrific. Like nothing I'd ever seen before. It was shorter than me and rounder – if it had

had two more arms it could have been some kind of nasty, giant insect.

"What's wrong?" The smile on Dad's face vanished, like a torch that had been switched off.

I looked at Mum. She frowned at me.

"I … nothing," I said.

But it was too late. Dad had read my face.

"Come on, Claire. Tell me what's wrong with it." Dad's voice was cold, angry.

"Why does it look like that?" I asked.

"Like what?" he snapped.

"So … so strange," I said. "It looks … I don't know. Round. And soft. And squashed."

"Ah! Now that's interesting," Dad said. He rubbed his hands together with glee. "My co-workers and I believe that technology in its current form has gone as far as it can. We need a brand-new way of working, and so we asked permission to experiment on some DNA from the Natural History Museum. We got hold of some DNA samples that were over 4,000 years old. Imagine that! 4,000 years old! We had a few false starts, but in the end we rebuilt the DNA. And that is how we developed what you see here."

Dad did everything but bow when he'd finished his speech. He reminded me of a proud peacock. I walked up to his project and prodded it with my finger. It felt like nothing I'd ever touched before.

"Why does it look so ... so horrible?" I couldn't help it. I had to say the word.

"What do you mean?" Dad said. "It's meant to be you!" Dad grinned. "I modelled her face on yours."

I stared at him. He must have lost his mind. This ... this thing was meant to be me? What an insult!

"Of course she's not an exact copy of you, but she's based on you," he said.

"I don't understand," I said. I wasn't sure I wanted to understand.

"I scanned your brain patterns to create her mind," Dad told me. "I wanted her to be able to reason things out for herself. So I decided to imprint your brain patterns into her processor. And it worked. She has a mind of her own."

My head was fizzing. "You used my brain patterns to create this?" I was appalled.

"Yes, of course," Dad said. "Remember a couple of months ago when I recorded your memories on the cogno-chip? Well, I used the data from that chip to create AI-E."

This was getting worse. AI-E stood in front of me, and its lips turned up in what I can only assume was a smile.

"Mark, Claire is right. Why does it look so ... so odd?" Mum asked Dad.

"Well, she's made of a new kind of material – like nothing we've ever seen before," Dad said. "And I found that the more she learned and thought, the more her processor grew. Imagine that! It got bigger and heavier. I didn't expect that at all. The material the processor is made of grows with it too."

Dad paused, like a teacher who wanted to check that his students were keeping up.

"Her processor is a brand-new design," he went on. "It's like nothing anyone's ever seen before. It's not like ours – it sends electrical and chemical signals. Isn't that fantastic? I never thought she could be this good, not even in my wildest dreams."

CHAPTER 5
DIFFERENT

I faded out as Dad droned on. I just stood and stared at AI-E. It stared back at me.

"So, Claire, what d'you think now?"

I faded in again as Dad said my name.

Dad had well and truly lost his mind. He'd gone too far this time. How could he? And he didn't ask my permission. How could he?

"That thing has really got my memories?" I asked.

"Only up until three months ago," Dad said. "The two of you have your own memories from that point on." He sounded cold and defensive again. "I didn't think you'd mind."

We both knew that was a lie. He knew how I'd feel, but he'd decided to go ahead anyway. And now it was done, there wasn't anything I could do about it, and he knew it. The same old story. It wasn't the first time and it wouldn't be the last.

"Is that all I am to you?" I asked. "A source of data for your projects?"

Dad didn't even bother to deny it. He just brushed my hurt aside. "Now, Claire, you're behaving like a child again," he said.

"I am a child – remember?" I told him.

"Well, thank goodness AI-E is more level-headed than you," Dad said. His voice had a sharp edge. He turned to the thing. "AI-E, say hello to my daughter Claire."

"Hello, Claire." Even AI-E's voice sounded strange. It wasn't like a normal voice at all. It was full of breath sounds and echoes. "I've been looking forward to meeting you," it said.

I still couldn't believe it. Dad had built a walking, talking computer with my brain patterns and what was meant to be my face. If I looked like AI-E, I'd walk around with a paper bag on my head.

"I don't like it, Dad," I said. "When are you going to shut it down?"

"Shut down AI-E?" Dad was stunned. "I've worked for years to perfect her and you want me to destroy her?"

"Dad, it's not real," I said.

"Not real?" he spluttered. "She's as real as you or me, Claire. And she's a 'she', not an 'it'!" He was shouting at me now. "AI-E can think for herself," he yelled. "I don't mean that she can follow patterns laid out in a program. I mean she can really think for herself. Analyse, reason, learn. I've even set up her room with access to the net so that she can watch and listen and learn about our world – and she's ahead of us already."

"Mum, do something," I begged. "Make him shut it down. Make him get rid of it."

Mum just stared at AI-E and shook her head.

Dad took a deep breath. "Claire, I really don't know what your problem is." He glared at me.

I didn't care.

He was acting as if I'd asked him to get rid of ... well, get rid of me.

No, I take that back. He wouldn't have made as much fuss if it was me he had to get rid of. Dad was given me. But he had made AI-E himself.

AI-E smiled at me. "Please, Claire," it said. "I am your friend. And you will always come first with Mark."

"Don't call my dad that," I said.

Dad sprang to AI-E's defence. "I told her to call me Mark," he said. "What else is she going to call me? Now if you can't be happy for me, Claire, you can leave. Go on. And I'll tell you something else. If AI-E were in your place, she wouldn't make all this fuss."

I couldn't take it any more. I just couldn't.

I dragged up the filthiest look I could and sent it towards Dad like a poison arrow.

Then I ran out of the lab.

CHAPTER 6
CONTROL

I sat in the car outside the lab and burned with a strange mix of envy and fear.

After a while, Mum joined me. She drove us home. We both sat in stony silence. As soon as we got home, I tried to run up to my room but Mum stopped me.

"Claire, I want to talk to you," she said.

"I don't want to talk to you or anyone else," I said.

"Tough!" Mum pulled then pushed me into the living room. "Sit down."

I sat down. All of a sudden I felt very tired and sad.

Mum put her arm around me and sighed.

"Claire, you're not as tough as you like to think you are," she said. "And I know your father can be a bit thoughtless sometimes. But that doesn't mean that you have to be that way too."

"What do you mean?" I sniffed.

"You were a bit ... blunt." Mum chose her words with care. "I know it was hard to hide what you felt when that ... thing was presented to us out of the blue like that. But you have to learn to keep quiet until you can control what you want to say and how you're going to say it."

"Like you do?" I asked.

"Like I do," Mum said, with another sigh. "I had to learn and so will you. That's what sets us apart from any other creatures. We can think without our feelings getting in the way. When you've learned to control what you do and say, then you're an adult. You have to learn to control your feelings until you no longer have them."

"Don't you have any feelings at all?" I asked.

Mum shook her head.

"Not even for me?" I wanted to ask, but the words wouldn't come.

"Will I be like you one day?" I asked instead.

"Of course!" she said.

"What about ... what about if you have other children?" I whispered.

"You're my daughter, Claire," Mum said. "Nothing will change that."

That wasn't the answer I was hoping for, but it would have to do.

"For now, you have to remember that you're Mark's daughter as well," Mum went on. "You must treat him with the proper respect."

"But why?" I demanded. "Why can't I tell Dad how I feel? He had no right to use me for his project."

"I agree," Mum said. "But there are ways to help him see that." She smiled. "There's an old saying – 'You can catch more flies with honey than with vinegar'."

CHAPTER 7
NIGHTMARE

I went up to my room to think about what Mum had said. I wanted to chat to Maisie about it. I knew Mum was right, but I still couldn't calm down. There was a strange kind of anger inside me, not hot, but cold. It burned its way through my body like ice.

To: Maisie@maisiemail.private.uk
From: Claire@clairemail.private.uk

Hello Maisie

I'm sorry I didn't reply to your last message right away but something came up. My dad –

the so-called genius – has invented what he calls 'the future'. He's built a walking, talking computer that can think for itself.

But my dad's a liar. All he did was copy my brain patterns into the thing and use my mind as the basis for its thoughts. Mum and I went to see it today. It was horrible. It had two legs and two arms like we do, but it's made of this weird springy, squashy material. Its eyes are like nothing I've ever seen before. Those eyes would give you nightmares for a month. And Dad had the cheek to say it was modelled on me. I hate it.

Dad doesn't realise he's created a monster. It's got to go. Watch this space.

Your friend
Claire

    I sat in front of the screen for a good ten minutes but Maisie didn't reply. For the first time I wished I could meet up with her in real life. I needed to talk to someone, really talk to someone who would understand how I felt about the way Dad treated me. When I looked at the AI-E, it was as if it was pulling Dad further and further away from me. I was sure that Maisie would understand.

I lay on my bed and stared up at the ceiling. I had some real thinking to do.

My screen bleeped and I jumped up off the bed.

To: Claire@clairemail.private.uk
From: Maisie@maisiemail.private.uk

Dear Claire

What are you going to do? Please don't do anything before you have time to think. I'm sure your father's new invention means you no harm. Why don't you try to get to know it first before you make up your mind to hate it?

I know that's easy for me to say because I'm not in your shoes, but I'm sure your dad loves you and would do anything to make you happy. I really think you don't know how lucky you are. I would give anything to be in your shoes. If I had one wish in the world it would be that I could get away from my father. I've never told anyone that but you. But I know I can trust you.

Please be careful. You're a true friend and I don't want to lose you. Take care.

Your friend
Maisie

My fingers flew across the keyboard after I'd read Maisie's message. I couldn't believe it. Of all people, she was on Dad's side!

Then I remembered something. I went back over the messages she'd sent me. There it was. I wondered why I hadn't picked up on it before.

I deleted the message I'd begun and started again.

To: Maisie@maisiemail.private.uk
From: Claire@clairemail.private.uk

Dear Maisie

You say that you wish you were in my shoes, but I don't think you really understand what my life is like. If you did, you wouldn't wish that.

You said in one of your messages that your dad hopes you'll make him rich one day. How are you meant to do that? Do you have some special talent or something? If you have, you kept that quiet!

Your dad must be a monster for you to envy me. Can't you go and live with other relatives? I'm sorry I didn't ask before. I guess I got caught up in what my dad was up to. But believe me, my dad really is horrible. He doesn't care about Mum and me. We're just two more of his fans, in his mind. I'm going to change all that. You just see if I don't.

Love
Claire

I touched 'Send', but in fact I didn't know how I was going to change things. I only knew I had to do something. I had to show Dad he couldn't treat Mum and me like this.

What could I do that would make Dad sit up and take notice of us? I leaned back in my chair and sighed. The only thing Dad had eyes for at the moment was AI-E.

So why not do something about AI-E?

The thought entered my head, and a plan followed right away.

Mum said honey was best, but I preferred vinegar.

I would make Dad realise just how lucky he was to have his family.

CHAPTER 8
ALONE

To: Claire@clairemail.private.uk
From: Maisie@maisiemail.private.uk

Dear Claire

Please, please stop and think before you do anything you'll regret. You're worrying me. What are you going to do? Whatever it is, maybe I can help you? After all, that's what friends are for. I think – I hope – I live close enough to you to be of some help. Let me know what you have in mind.

Your friend
Maisie

I smiled when I read Maisie's message and sent a reply straight away.

To: Maisie@maisiemail.private.uk
From: Claire@clairemail.private.uk

Dear Maisie

Thanks for your last message but I think I can do this alone. Don't worry.

I'm going to teach Dad a lesson. Tonight, when Mum's asleep, I'm going to go to his lab and I'm going to sort out the AI-E.

I know Dad will be at the lab but he won't be in his office all the time. I'm going to get rid of the AI-E. It's not made of the same stuff as us so it shouldn't be too difficult. I don't know how Dad can say it's more advanced than us when it's made of something so soft and squidgy. Its processor might be amazing but what good is that when the shell is so soft? I'm going to see just how soft it is tonight.

Wish me luck.

Your friend
Claire

    I went offline after that. I didn't want
Maisie to try and talk me out of it. I had to do
this.

    It was the AI-E or me.

CHAPTER 9
CHOICE

I looked at my watch as I stood outside Dad's lab. 11.30 p.m. I couldn't turn back now, even if I wanted to – which I didn't. Mum had shut down for the night but if I went back home now, she'd instantly wake up. I didn't want that to happen. Not if I didn't have anything to show for it.

I walked around the back of the building and used Dad's spare key card to let myself in. The building was dark and quiet. I knew the two security guards would be at the front, watching TV. I also knew that between 11 p.m.

and midnight, Dad always went to the rest room in the basement to recharge his power cell.

So I had half an hour – or 20 minutes if I wanted to be on the safe side. I ran up five flights of stairs rather than take the lift and swiped myself into Dad's lab. I forced myself not to think about the months and years Dad had spent working on AI-E. It came down to a simple choice. Dad's project or Dad's family.

It was so bright – every light in the place must've been on. But it was also so quiet that it was creepy. I looked around. The place was empty.

15 minutes left …

I didn't want to get this wrong.

I crept across the floor to the lab next door. That had to be where Dad kept the AI-E. She'd come out of that lab when Mum and I had first

seen her. I opened the lab door – and gasped.
The last time I'd seen this lab, it had been full
of work-benches covered in tools and wires and
gadgets.

Now it was like someone's bedroom. There
was a simple bed against the wall and opposite
that was a desk with screen above it. The
screen was on and it was connected to the net.

CHAPTER 10
FATHER

"Hello, Claire."

My head whipped round. The AI-E was standing there watching me. It smiled and its whole face wrinkled up. I couldn't help it. I took a step back.

"I've been waiting for you," the AI-E said.

"What're you talking about?" My eyes narrowed. It was clear the thing was trying to creep me out. "You couldn't have known I was coming," I said.

"You told me." AI-E smiled and pointed to the screen above the desk. "Look for yourself if you don't believe me."

I kept a wary eye on the AI-E as I walked over to the screen. I was astonished to see the last message I'd sent to Maisie, there on the screen.

"What … How did you get that message?" I demanded. "I sent that to my friend, not you. How dare you …?"

"You sent it to me," the AI-E said.

"Yeah right!" I yelled. "Since when is your name Maisie and … how did …?" I trailed off and stared at the AI-E.

"Mark's Artificial Intelligence Sample Incarnation Experiment – or Maisie for short," the AI-E said.

"I … I don't believe it …" I gabbled.

"I told you not to do anything before you stopped to think." The AI-E started walking towards me.

I stumbled backwards. "What're you going to do?" I asked.

"Talk to you. Reason with you," the AI-E said.

I didn't take my eyes off the thing. I didn't realise I was backing away until I backed into the wall opposite the door and jarred my body. AI-E stood in front of me, so close I could hear the strange sound of her breath.

"Touch me," the AI-E ordered. "Go on. Touch my hand."

I tried to put my hands behind my back but the AI-E pulled them out and held my hands in her own.

"I know my skin isn't made of metal like yours, but does that really make me so dreadful?" AI-E asked. "I wish I did have a metal skin instead of this soft ... stuff, but that's how Father made me."

"Father?" I repeated.

"Your dad is my dad," the AI-E said. "He made me. I'm a life form based on carbon. I have something called 'blood' running through me because the organs inside my body need oxygen to survive. The blood takes oxygen around my body and helps my body to repair itself. I work a different way from you but I still feel and think – just as you do."

I stopped trying to pull my hand away from hers. Her skin felt so strange – warm and springy. I looked down at my own hand. Dull grey metal gleamed back at me.

"Father calls me the next stage in technology. He calls me the future," the AI-E said. "I can think and analyse just like you can, but I can also dream – something you have never been able to do. I can adapt my own programming and I have my own ideas. They come out of something Father calls my 'imagination'."

"And I suppose you think this all makes you better than normal people?" I scowled. "Better than androids like me?"

"Not better. Just different," the AI-E said.

"Why didn't you tell me who you were when we talked online?" I asked. "Why did you lie?"

"I didn't lie," the AI-E said. "Your father calls me AI-E. I made up the name Maisie myself. And I do think of us as sisters. After all, Father gave me your memories, so I was you. Then I began to think for myself and my thoughts and feelings became my own. But up until then, my memories are your memories."

I watched Maisie. She watched me.

"Your DNA? Where did it come from?" I asked.

"I've spent the last few weeks finding that out," Maisie said. "I hacked into the government systems and found some top-secret files. It seems that there were millions of life forms like me on Earth many thousands of years ago. We invented androids but then a virus killed us all off and you androids were all that were left. I guess you had to fend for yourselves and so your thinking developed. But you didn't want to remember that you were made, so the information was kept secret."

"You made us?" I couldn't believe it.

"I have no reason to lie about it," Maisie said, her voice sad. "Now do you see why I envy you? You have a mother and father and friends who are like you. I call Mark 'Father', but he never was my father and we both know it.

Claire, everywhere you look there are others like you. But look at me. I'm thousands of years too late. I'm all alone."

And, for the first time, I began to wonder what it must be like to be Maisie.

"Are you still going to destroy me?" Maisie asked. "If you want to, I'll let you. You're the first one who's treated me like a real person rather than an experiment. But now that you know what I really am ..."

"I was going to lock you in and burn this place down," I said. "You weren't a person to me, you were just a thing. I thought if Dad didn't have you any more, then maybe he'd come back to Mum and me."

"And now?" Maisie asked.

That was the question. What was I going to do now?

CHAPTER 11
FIRE

It was all over the news. Stories about the tragic loss of the lab and all the research data. The world was filled with pity for Mark Drayton, Android 45902-X45-TAG4039, my father.

The loss of the research materials was bad, but the loss of AI-E was worse. Dad and his co-workers tried to find bits of her in the hope they could save something. But the AI-E was an organic life form, not a metal unit, and so there was no trace of her left. That's what they all

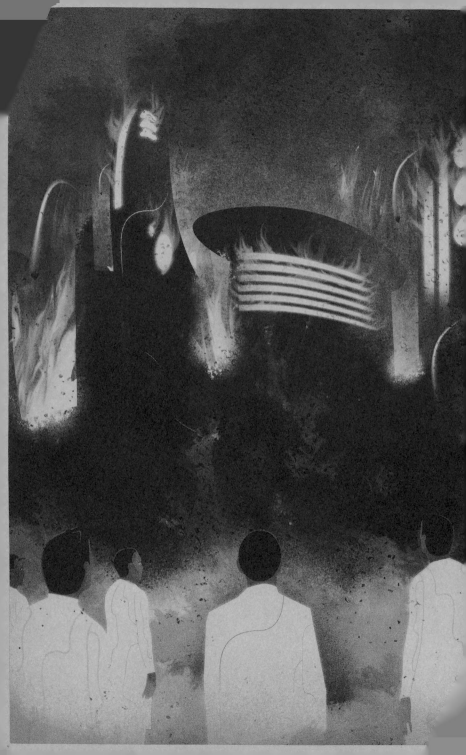

thought. And since Dad had lost his research data, he was back to square one.

I think the fire destroyed something in Dad as well. After that, all his love for his work faded. He'd been knocked back too far to start again. I don't think he could face more years of research, more jigsaws of ancient DNA before he'd have anything like the AI-E again.

I didn't mean for Dad to stop working. I didn't want him to come back to Mum and me that way. Maisie and I just wanted it to look as if Maisie had been destroyed in the blaze.

At first I was very upset about Dad, but I find that the sadness I feel grows smaller every day. This time next year, I don't expect to feel anything at all. Mum and Dad were right. My feelings are disappearing. I'm growing up at last.

CHAPTER 12
DREAMS

CLAIRE DRAYTON, Android 39028-X46-TAG4054
PERSONAL LOG: DATE: 8 FEBRUARY 7504 AD

I only feel about two things now. One is Maisie.
The other is the thought of having a child of
my own. I look forward to having the chance
to imprint my brain patterns on an infant unit.
I'll do a better job than my dad did with me.

I've got Maisie hidden where no one will
find her. We saved as many of Dad's research
notes as we could and I've promised Maisie
that I'll do my best to take Dad's work forward

when I get older. I'll be a scientist like him and create a partner for Maisie.

Maisie doesn't want to be the only one of her kind anywhere in the world. It would be great to create more humanoids like Maisie. Dad was right about how wonderful she is. Her processor is equal to mine and then some. She calls it a 'brain'. I enjoy listening to her talk. Some of the things she talks about make me envy her – like the patterns she sees in the clouds, and her dreams. She can make up stories on the spur of the moment that have no basis in truth. It seems as natural to her as breathing. I'm beginning to understand why Dad was so obsessed with her.

As for Maisie, she often asks about Dad. When I tell her how he sits at home and stares at the walls, the strangest thing happens. Her face gets very wet. She calls it 'crying'.

Maisie may be the smartest piece of tech kit in the world, but she has feelings. And from the look of it, her feelings are never going to pass. She'll never grow out of them. Unlike me.

And so I wonder ...

Should I try to make the next humanoid so that it grows out of its feelings, like I will?

Who is better? Me, who cannot love, or Maisie, who loves too much?